WELCOME
to
SILVER STREET
FARM

WELCOME
to
SILVER STREET
FARM

NICOLA DAVIES
illustrated by Katharine McEwen

CANDLEWICK PRESS

Copyright © 2011 by Nicola Davies
Illustrations copyright © 2011 by Katharine McEwen

First U.S. paperback edition 2013

Library of Congress Catalog Card Number 2012942670

ISBN 978-0-7636-5831-1 (hardcover)
ISBN 978-0-7636-6443-5 (paperback)

14 15 16 17 18 BVG 10 9 8 7 6 5 4 3

Printed in Berryville, VA, U.S.A.

This book was typeset in Stempel Schneidler and Cows.
The illustrations were done in pen and watercolor.

Candlewick Press
99 Dover Street
Somerville, Massachusetts 02144

visit us at www.candlewick.com

For Joseph and Gabriel
and the real Flinty

A MAP OF SILVER STREET FARM

Main gate

Scrub

Ticket office

Waiting room

Ladies waiting room

Platform

Railway tracks

N

CANAL

Chapter One

Gemma says that it started with eating jelly beans on the merry-go-round in the park. Karl says no, it started with Auntie Nat's poodles. But Meera knows that the *real* beginning of Silver Street Farm was their very first day of kindergarten in Mrs. Monty's class.

On that first day of school, the only children who weren't screaming, crying, or having a nosebleed were a tall girl with red braids, a quiet, skinny boy with dark hair, and Meera.

Mrs. Monty led them to the play area in the corner of the classroom.

"Could you three play nicely with the toy town," she said, "while I sort everything else out? There are some farm animals, too, in that red box."

Meera was lifting the lid off the red box almost before Mrs. Monty had finished speaking; but she wasn't alone. The two other children were right beside her. Just like her, they weren't in the least bit interested in the fancy toy town laid out all around them. It was the farm animals they wanted to play with.

"I'm Meera," said Meera, smiling shyly.

"I'm Gemma," said the tall girl with red braids.

"I'm Karl," said the skinny boy very quietly. "Do you want to play farm?"

For the rest of the day, while Mrs. Monty wrestled with classroom chaos, the three new best friends built their first farm together. They got out all the animals, even the two cows with legs missing, the headless sheep, and the chickens that had been painted pink. They made stables, stalls, and sties from old cereal boxes and new fences from lollipop sticks and yellow yarn. Very soon, fields and farm buildings, flocks of sheep, and herds of cows and pigs had sprung up among the buildings and roads of the toy town.

The three children worked well together. Gemma liked the sheep and the chickens best; Karl didn't say much, but you could tell he liked the cows and the horses. Meera was always having ideas about what to do next, but Gemma and Karl didn't mind because she wasn't *really* bossy and she had found the missing piglets at the bottom of the LEGO box.

When Mrs. Monty asked them to put the farm away because it was time to go home, the children were horrified.

"But I have to milk the cows in the morning," said Karl.

"And the sheep can't graze if they're in a *box*," said Gemma.

"But tomorrow the other children will want to play with the toy town," said Mrs. Monty gently.

"They can play with the town *and* the farm together!" said Gemma.

"You see," Meera explained kindly, "it's a *city* farm. It fits in the city, just like the farm *we're* all going to have when we're older."

From that moment on, Meera, Gemma,

and Karl planned their real city farm. They read books about farm animals, and they went on every school trip and family outing they could to real farms to see and learn about real animals. All through kindergarten and right through to the last year of elementary school, the three friends planned—but still their city farm was just a dream. Until, that is, the day of the green jelly beans and Auntie Nat's poodles.

Chapter Two

Gemma and Karl were lying on the old merry-go-round in the park, eating jelly beans and looking up into the blue spring sky over Lonchester.

"Give us a push, Gem," said Karl. "We're stopping."

Gemma kicked out lazily at the concrete with one of her superlong legs and started the merry-go-round turning again.

Karl bit a yellow jelly bean in half and sighed.

"April vacation at home with nothing to do but watch Auntie Nat read horoscopes. . . ."

"I'd swap you a year with your auntie's horoscopes for two weeks with my pimply brother."

Gemma gave them another push and the merry-go-round creaked on. "Where is Meera, anyway?" she said through a mouthful of red jelly beans. "She said to meet at three o'clock and it's twenty after now."

"I'm right here!" Meera ran out of the trees and jumped onto the merry-go-round, sending it spinning wildly. "And I've got some good news. This could be the year we start our farm!"

From either side of her, Karl and Gemma both groaned.

"Meera, we don't have any animals," said Karl.

"And if we *did* have any animals, where would we keep them?" added Gemma. "My dad's toolshed?"

"Or the balcony of Auntie's apartment?" added Karl.

"But if we *did* have somewhere to keep them," said Meera, sitting bolt upright, "that would be a start, wouldn't it?"

"But finding somewhere is the difficult part," said Karl gloomily. "We've always known that."

"Well," said Meera, her eyes starting to sparkle, "I think I *have* found somewhere! My Auntie Priya works in the city-council offices and she told me about it. There's an old railway station down by the canal that's been closed for years. There are buildings to keep animals in and grassy parts for grazing. It sounds perfect."

"But the city council would never let us have a place like that," said Gemma.

"It's probably just ruins covered in brambles," added Karl.

Meera ignored their objections. "It can't hurt to go and have a look though, can it?" she said.

But Gemma and Karl still looked doubtful.

"I know!" said Meera, leaping off the merry-go-round. "Let the jelly beans decide!" She snatched the bag from Gemma and struck a pose like an actor on a stage.

"I veel close my eyes. I veel hold out zee magical bag of jelly beans. . . ." Meera paused dramatically. Peeking between her eyelashes,

she could see that Karl and Gemma were now both watching her and starting to laugh — she'd *gotten* them! — "And if zee next jelly bean I pull from zee bag eez *green,* you veel be bound by jelly-bean magic to accompany me on my quest for our farm!"

Meera pointed in Karl's direction.

"Drumroll please, Karl!"

Karl drummed his fingers on the old merry-go-round, and Gemma provided a trumpet fanfare with a rolled-up newspaper she had found.

Meera reached into the bag with her other hand, paused dramatically, and pulled out . . . a green jelly bean!

"Ta-da!"

Karl and Gemma clapped and got off the

merry-go-round. Sometimes, you just had to do what Meera wanted, even if you knew that the jelly bean *had* to be green because none of them liked the lime-flavored ones.

Chapter Three

Auntie Nat blinked. She looked at the screen again. It couldn't be true, could it?

"Adorable poodles. Two left. Bargain for quick sale."

The photo on the advertisement was terribly blurred, but then dogs moved around so much, didn't they? They'd be hard to photograph. She wrote down the number on the screen and, her heart pounding with excitement, reached for the phone.

Auntie Nat, or Natalia Konstantinovna Lebedeva, to give her her proper name, had always wanted a pair of white poodles with ribbons tied into their woolly fur.

"I walk with them to shops," she would tell Karl in her heavy Russian accent. "And I look elegant, like models in magazine."

Then she'd walk across the living room, pretending to be a tall, skinny model with two dogs on leashes. This always made Karl and Auntie Nat laugh, because she was short and very, very round.

"When I'm rich and famous, Auntie," Karl always said, "I'll buy you two perfect little poodles."

"Ah, my Karl," she'd sigh, "you will have to be very rich. Poodles *so* expensive."

Poodles *were* so expensive, hundreds and hundreds of dollars. Every week, when she was reading her horoscope in the *Lonchester Herald* and on the Mythic Modes website, she'd check online in case someone, somewhere, was selling a poodle for a price she could afford. But the stars always told her that wasn't going to happen. Until today.

"A long-held dream is closer than you think!" said her horoscope on the back page of the *City Gazette*.

The voice at the end of the phone line was gruff.

"Yeah, I still got the dogs," it said. "You got the money?"

Hmmm, Auntie Nat thought to herself. *Not a refined person. Not good enough to own fine poodles.*

"Yes, yes," she said carefully, "I have money. Cash."

"Right. Then meet me at the corner of Milsom Street and Park Row in an hour."

He didn't even wait for her to reply. Perhaps the puppies were stolen. Auntie Nat pushed the worrying thought to the back of her mind and, thinking instead of what Karl would say when he got home and found two little poodle puppies in the apartment, almost skipped down the hall to the creaking, cranking old elevator.

The man was definitely not a refined person. In fact, he looked as if he could use a bath. What was more, he seemed to be in a great rush to get rid of the puppies. He shoved the box into Auntie Nat's hands and told her that the puppies were sleeping and that it would be better not to open the box until she got home. This had made her suspicious, but when she'd poked a finger in through an airhole in the box, she'd felt the warm, woolly fur. She handed over the money and hurried home.

Back in the apartment, Auntie Nat brought the box into the kitchen and sat down gratefully on a chair. She looked at it, but she didn't open it. Now that her long-held dream was about to come true, as the horoscope had predicted, she realized that she didn't really know anything about poodles. They were cute and fluffy, but what did they eat? How did you train them? Where, she thought with sudden horror, did they "do their business"?

Inside the pet carrier, the pups were starting to wake up and move around. She would have to let them out. She opened the top of the box, and two sweet little white woolly faces looked up at her and opened their mouths.

"Baa!" said the puppies. "Baaaaaaaa!"

Chapter Four

The old station was most definitely *not* open to visitors: the huge wrought-iron gates were closed with a giant chain and padlock and covered in signs that shouted fiercely, NO ENTRY! and TRESPASSERS WILL BE PROSECUTED! and, most worrying of all, DANGER! GUARD DOGS PATROLLING AT ALL TIMES.

"We can't go in there!" said Karl.

"Yes, we can!" said Meera.

"What about the guard dogs?" asked Gemma.

"Oh, that's just for show," said Meera, waving her hands dismissively.

Karl, who was still small for his age, looked up at the gate.

"How will we get in?"

"Climb, of course. Duh!" said Meera.

Gemma laughed. "But you're terrible at climbing, Meera!"

"That's where you come in, Daddy Long-legs. Get up there, Gemma!"

Gemma *was* the best climber of the three of them, and she could never resist a challenge.

"OK. I'll get on top of the gate, then I'll help you guys up," she said. "And if we get thrown in jail, at least I won't have to spend all vacation with my brother."

Once they were on top of the gates, it was easy to slide down the other side and start to explore. There were several old brick buildings, some with faded signs still hanging above them: TICKET OFFICE, WAITING ROOM, and STATION-MASTER'S OFFICE. The windows were broken and there was ivy growing up the walls, but the roofs still looked solid and weatherproof. The space around the buildings was big, about half the size of the school soccer field, Karl guessed. It was completely overgrown, but where brambles and nettles would grow, so would grass for animals to graze. As the children wandered around, the dreams they'd had since the first day of kindergarten finally seemed within their reach.

They pushed through the jungle of plants and at last reached the edge of the canal, where they sat down with their legs dangling over the wall.

"It's brilliant!" said Gemma. "I think there could be enough grazing in summer for a couple of sheep."

"The ticket office would make a great cowshed," said Karl.

"We could have ducks on the canal," said Gemma, "once we've gotten the shopping cart out, of course."

That was when they heard the growl and turned around to see a huge black dog with a row of very big teeth showing in an extremely fierce snarl.

"Just for show, eh?" said Gemma.

"Nice doggy. Nice, nice, *nice* doggy," breathed Meera.

The "doggy" wasn't impressed; he snarled

and growled some more and began to close in.

"We'll have to jump into the canal if he gets any closer," said Gemma.

"We'll be stabbed by a rusty shopping cart!" squealed Meera.

"Meera, quick!" said Karl. "Give me the jelly beans!"

Two minutes later, the "fierce" guard dog was wagging his tail and begging for more candy. Karl scratched him behind the ears.

"There's a good boy," said Karl.

The dog whined and offered his paw.

"I think he's lonely," said Gemma.

"He won't be lonely when he's the Silver Street Farm Dog!" said Meera as she patted the dog's huge head.

"The *what* farm dog?" Gemma and Karl said together.

"Oh, I forgot to tell you! I found this nailed to the back of an old bench. It's the station name." Meera reached into her backpack and pulled out an enamel sign that said SILVER STREET in black letters. "It's perfect for our farm."

"Silver Street Farm," said Karl. "Yeah, I like it."

"Silver Street sounds a bit like a shopping center to me," Gemma said, grinning. "But it's OK."

They fought their way back through the bramble jungle and climbed out over the gate. The dog stuck his nose through the bars and they fed him one last green jelly bean. He wagged his tail at them as they walked away.

"I think he knows we're coming back!" said Gemma.

Chapter Five

As soon as Karl opened the door to the apartment, he knew something was wrong. There was a horrible smell, for a start, and he could hear his auntie speaking angrily in Russian in the living room. Then he noticed the newspapers spread all over the floor, decorated with little brown currants and round damp patches. He didn't have to wonder what had been pooping and peeing all over his home for long though, because just as he closed the front door behind him, two fluffy little lambs ran into the hall.

"Baaa!" said the lambs. "*Baaaaaaaaaaa!*"

Auntie Nat was following close behind, bending over the lambs and offering them food from a bowl with DOG written on the side.

"Ah, Karl!" Auntie Nat looked at him with a big smile. "At last, I have poodles. Puppies. Bargain from Internet."

"Baaaaaa!" said the "puppies" together, more loudly than ever.

"This one," said Auntie Nat, pointing to the larger lamb, "is Bitzi, and the other one, little one, is Bobo."

Karl nodded. He didn't know what to say. Auntie Nat waved the dog bowl around.

"I get puppy food," she said, "but they don't like." Auntie Nat's beaming smile faded. "If they don't eat, they die," she said. Suddenly she looked almost as forlorn as the lambs.

"Don't worry, Auntie," said Karl, finding his voice at last, "I'll figure it out."

The baby bottles were the easy part. Mr. Khan's corner shop had them hanging up behind the counter, next to the aspirin and Band-Aids. Karl chose two. But what to put *in* the bottles was much trickier.

He spent ages looking at the cartons of milk in the cooler. There was skim, low-fat, and organic—but none of them were sheep's milk. He peered into the freezer, but saw nothing that seemed to have anything to do with sheep apart from a package of frozen lamb chops.

When he got to the checkout, one of Mr. Khan's nephews was at the register.

"Excuse me," said Karl. "Do you have any other kinds of milk?"

"What?" said the young man, scowling.

"Milk from—um—other animals."

"What d'you mean, *other animals*?" the boy said, scowling even more. "Are you making fun of me?"

Just as Karl was wishing that the floor would swallow him up, Mr. Khan himself appeared.

"Ah!" he said kindly, sweeping his grumpy nephew to one side. "Karl! How is your aunt?"

"She's well, thanks, Mr. Khan."

"And you were looking for?"

Karl was aware that now everyone in the line was listening to him.

"Sheep's milk, Mr. Khan," Karl said in a very small voice, expecting the shopkeeper to burst into laughter or throw him out for being rude.

"Sheep's milk. Yes," said Mr. Khan, as if it

were the most normal thing in the world. "So good for the digestion. Also for complaints of the skin. Your aunt is quite well, I hope?"

For a split second, Karl thought of explaining about the poodle puppies that were really sheep, but it was much easier to just say, "She's fine, Mr. Khan. Just a bit of eczema."

"Well, we can't have that. Please come this way."

Mr. Khan rummaged around in the freezer and pulled out a bag of frozen whitish stuff about the size of a soccer ball.

"Mr. Stephanopolis, may he rest in peace, ordered sheep's milk every week. I hope your aunt finds it beneficial."

Back at the apartment, Karl defrosted the milk in the microwave, put some in each of the bottles, and together he and Auntie Nat fed the lambs. Karl showed Auntie how to hold the bottle, just as he'd been taught on a school trip to a farm back in third grade.

The lambs braced their little legs and sucked hard at the teats, their tiny tails wiggling like demented pipe cleaners. When the bottles had been sucked dry, the lambs became sleepy. Auntie Nat picked up Bobo, and Karl took Bitzi onto his lap; the lamb nibbled at his sleeve and closed its eyes with pleasure as he scratched its nubbly little head.

"So cute!" said Auntie Nat, smiling. Karl nodded and smiled back. They *were* cute. They were *gorgeous,* but in a minute he was going to have to tell Auntie Nat that they *weren't* puppies, and he didn't know how he was going to do it.

"Karl," said his auntie, gently stroking a

lamb under the chin, "while you are out, I look on Internet. I check pictures of poodles. These are not poodles. These are sheeps."

Karl sighed.

"Yes, Auntie. I know."

"You think I am foolish?"

"No, Auntie. You've never seen a poodle up close." said Karl. "And anyway," he added, "there's nothing foolish about having a dream."

Chapter Six

While Karl was delving into the freezer with Mr. Khan, Gemma was sweeping fur and fluff from the floor of the vet's waiting room.

She worked there two evenings a week, mostly cleaning, but sometimes she got to help with the animals.

"Gemma!" Dr. Sweeney stepped into the waiting room. Gemma liked old Dr. Sweeney.

Of all the vets, he let her work with the animals the most. He was holding a small basket with five pale blue eggs inside.

"Mrs. Tasker brought them in for me. She knows I like duck eggs," said Dr. Sweeney. "But, bless her, she's a bit loopy, and I'm pretty sure they're rotten. Can you chuck them in the green trash can on your way out?"

"Yes," Gemma said, "of course."

"Thanks, Gemma. Next time I have to hold a hamster down, you're the one I'll call!" He grinned through his beard and went back to the exam room.

Gemma looked at the eggs. They didn't look bad. In fact, they looked beautiful, resting in a little nest of snowy feathers. She couldn't bear to chuck them in the trash can and hear them smash on the bottom. Very carefully, she wrapped the eggs in her sweatshirt and went home.

In the middle of the night, a tiny sound woke Gemma up.

Peep!

Then, *Peep! Peep!*

The sounds were coming from under her sweatshirt on the floor. The eggs! She'd been so busy all evening being annoyed by her brother, Lee, that she'd forgotten all about them.

She got out of bed and, very gently, pulled back the sweatshirt and peered at the eggs. A little flake of shell had fallen from the middle of the biggest one, and a beak, a patch of pink skin, and some wet yellow fluff showed through the hole. The eggs weren't rotten—they were just ready to hatch!

"Peep! Peep!" called the duckling from inside.

"Peep!" called another duckling from a different egg. Another flake of shell came off one of the other eggs with a tiny *crack,* and there was such a chorus of peeping that Gemma couldn't tell which eggs were talking and which weren't. Very gently, she lifted one to her ear and listened. Up against her ear she could hear little tapping sounds as the duckling's beak worked at the inside of its shelly prison.

"Hello!" she whispered.

"Peep!" the duckling answered softly. Gemma was so surprised that she almost dropped the egg. She tried again, a little louder this time.

"Hello!" she said.

"Peep!" replied the duckling.

Gemma spoke to the other eggs one by one, until she'd had a little conversation with all five of them. Then she sat with the basket on her lap and watched as more and more flakes of shell fell off. One of the eggs split right around the middle! The duckling inside slowly pushed the two halves apart and then struggled up on its leathery webbed feet. It shook its beak and looked right at her with its bright, dark eyes.

"Hello, duckling!" said Gemma.

"Peep, peep," said the duckling. It was wet and bedraggled looking, and Gemma realized that it would soon get very cold if it didn't dry out. She got a cardboard box down from her closet, lined it with old newspapers, and put her desk lamp on the floor so that its warm

bulb could shine inside the box and heat up the air.

By the time she got back to the ducklings, the first one had four little damp companions! She put them all inside the box to get warm, and they peep-peeped anxiously.

"Hush, ducklings!" Gemma soothed, and as she spoke to them, they settled down. The ducklings all sat on their feet and closed their eyes in the warmth of the lamp, like sunbathers. Soon they were drying out and becoming as yellow and fluffy as ducklings on an Easter card.

Gemma knew that newly hatched chicks didn't need to eat or drink for a few hours, so she didn't need to worry about feeding them until the morning. She pulled the box and lamp

close to her bed so she could check on the ducklings and speak to them in the night. Then she fell back into bed.

"Night, night, Silver Street Ducks," Gemma whispered sleepily as she closed her eyes.

"Peep, peep, peep, peep," the ducklings whispered back.

Chapter Seven

The next morning, Meera ran all the way to the park, where she was meeting Karl, Gemma, and the very first Silver Street livestock. Karl was already there with the lambs. They were wearing leashes and looked *a lot* like puppies.

"I had to carry them some of the way," said Karl, "but they don't seem to mind the collars and leashes at all."

Gemma arrived a few moments later with the ducklings tucked up in the hem of her T-shirt.

"They won't let me out of their sight," she said with a giggle. "I had to take them in the shower with me this morning!"

The children sat on the grass while the ducklings waddled around between their legs and the lambs took turns nibbling their hair and butting them playfully. It was hard to stop smiling and concentrate.

"The problem is," Gemma said, "Mom says I can't keep the ducklings. I've got to find them a home by the end of the week."

"Yeah," said Karl. "Now that Auntie Nat

knows they're sheep, she doesn't really want them in the apartment. You can't housebreak lambs. The whole place smells of sheep poop!"

"We need Silver Street right *now*!" Gemma said.

"But it could take months or even years to persuade the city council that a city farm is a good idea," said Karl, taking his hair out of Bobo's mouth.

"Hmmm," said Meera thoughtfully. "What we need is publicity."

"Yes!" said Karl. "If we get everybody in Lonchester on our side, then the city council would *have* to give us Silver Street."

"Cosmic TV!" said Gemma. "They're always asking for community stories."

Meera jumped up. "And these are *brilliant* stories . . . the great poodle-lamb swindle and the rotten eggs that turned into ducklings! Come on, if we walk across the park now, we might be in time for their morning news."

Sashi, the young reporter at Cosmic TV, was delighted. It was the best story they'd had in months, she said. Within five minutes, the children and the animals were lined up in the studio. It wasn't much more than a broom closet with lights, but it didn't matter. Meera and Karl held a lamb each, and the five ducklings popped their heads out of Gemma's T-shirt.

"Looks good!" said Stewy the cameraman, peering through his dreadlocks with a grin. "Looks really, *really* good!"

"If we get this right," said Meera, "the city council should give us Silver Street Farm tied up with a ribbon!"

"OK, everybody!" said Sashi. "On air in five, four . . ." she counted the last three seconds with her fingers.

A little red light lit up on Stewy's camera.

Sashi smiled into the camera and began to speak: "Three Lonchester children have big plans to make the derelict station at Silver Street into Lonchester's first city farm," she told the camera. "The city council may have other plans for the old station, but two extraordinary twists of fate have given the children a head start with *their* plans and provided them with their first farm animals!"

Then Sashi asked Karl about the poodle-lambs and how Auntie Nat had been tricked, while he and Meera fed the lambs with a bottle. Sashi asked Gemma about the "rotten" eggs that the vet was going to throw out, which had hatched into ducklings, while Gemma held a duckling and stroked its fluffy yellow head.

Then Sashi turned to Meera. "Why do you want to make Silver Street Station into a city farm?" she asked.

For a moment, Meera's head swam with all the dreams and plans that she and Gemma and Karl had made since they were small. Then, suddenly, she knew just what to say.

"Ever since we were in kindergarten, we've dreamed about making a farm in the city," she began. "We want all Lonchester children to come to Silver Street Farm and see what farm animals are like, so that no one grows up thinking that eggs and milk comes from a carton."

"Well, you heard it here first!" said Sashi. "More from Cosmic TV News at three."

The red light went off.

"That was brilliant, kids!" said Sashi. "This story is going to be *so* big!"

"Yeah! Big! *So* big," said Stewy. "Can I hold a duckling now?"

Chapter Eight

Sashi was right. The story spread through the city like wildfire.

Within hours, every TV and radio station was talking about it. Rockin' Roland Rogers, Lonchester City FM's most famous DJ, even hosted a call-in about it.

"So," said Rockin' Roland, "Mrs. O from Hopdown Flats, what would *you* like to say about these crazy kids and their plan to make old Silver Street Station into a farm?"

"I think it's wonderful," said Mrs. O in a shaky, old lady's voice. "It's not just the youngsters who would enjoy having farm animals at Silver Street. Us old folks would love it, too!"

"Jack Flash now on line three," said Rockin' Roland.

"It's, like, brilliant," said Jack. "Totally cool. I mean, the poodles being sheep, that was bad, but now kinda good. Yeah? Like, wow!"

"And just one more call. Hello, Jody on line two."

"If the council doesn't give Silver Street Station to the kids, I won't vote for them," said Jody, sounding very determined.

"Fighting talk there, Jody. And now for some music. The new single from Fake Tat—"

But the children didn't have time to watch

TV or listen to the radio, because soon after the very first broadcast on Cosmic TV, things got busy.

Meera, Gemma, and Karl were all at Gemma's house, so that the lambs could run around on the tiny patch of lawn and the ducklings could swim in the old wading pool, when Meera's cell phone rang. The only people who ever called her cell were Karl and Gemma, so it was a bit of a shock.

"Hello, Meera speaking!" said Meera, trying to sound grown-up.

"Hi Meera. It's Sashi from Cosmic TV." She sounded very stressed. "I think you guys need to get back down here. Somebody's just delivered ten bales of hay and"—Sashi took a deep breath—"some chickens and *two real live goats*!"

*   *   *

The sidewalk outside Cosmic TV was blocked with a pet carrier full of clucking chickens and a huge pile of hay bales. Standing on top of the bales, contentedly munching hay, were two goats. One was pure white with sticking-up ears, and the other was chocolate brown with droopy ears.

"Wow!" said Gemma, who had been reading up about goat breeds. "A Saanen and a Nubian!"

But before the children had time to say hello to Silver Street's first goats, Sashi rushed up looking very worried.

"We're in trouble," she said, and pointed to a very large, very round police officer who was standing by the hay bales. "I think you'd better speak to him."

Nervously, the three children approached

the officer. Close up, they could see that he was even bigger and angrier than he had at first appeared, but the moment he saw the children, the lambs, and the ducklings, his face broke into a big beaming smile.

"Ah!" he said, as if seeing the children and their animals was the biggest treat of his day. "I wondered when you'd get here!"

The police officer held out a huge hand for the children to shake. "I'm Sergeant Short," he said. "And I presume you're the youngsters who want to turn Silver Street Station into a city farm?"

Caught in Sergeant Short's blue-eyed stare, the children could only nod.

"Well," he said quietly, leaning down from his great height so that they could hear him whisper, "strictly off the record, I think that's a great idea, but"—he straightened up to his official height again—"we can't have goats and bales obstructing the public highway. So, my fellow officers and I will help you to get it all moved." And the sergeant gave the children the biggest wink they'd ever seen.

Sergeant Short asked Sashi not to film the hay bales, chickens, lambs, goats, and ducklings being loaded into the back of a big police van by four police officers.

"Not sure how the police chief would see it, really," he said. "Best keep it between us, eh?"

"Hop in!" said a young woman police officer with a big smile. She helped the children into the van, and they were off.

The children were too astonished to ask where they were being taken. Karl wondered anxiously if it was all just a trick and if they were about to go to prison. But when the doors opened, they found themselves at the far end of the park. The police had built a little compound for the animals using crash barriers and crowd-control netting.

In just a few minutes, the goats were happily nibbling hay and the chickens were scratching in the shade of the trees.

"You can't stay here long," said the sergeant, "but I've cleared it with the police chief until tomorrow. In the meantime, Julie—I mean Officer Worthing—will help keep an eye on things."

Julie leaned out of the driver's seat of the van.

"Sarge? Sarge! You need to see this!"

On a tiny television in the front of the police van, the Wire TV lunchtime news was just ending.

"We now bring you a live announcement from Lonchester City Council," the newscaster was saying. The picture cut to a big man in a suit, standing outside of City Hall.

He looked *very* angry.

"I would like to read the following statement from Lonchester City Council," the man began, already rather red in the face. "The council has for some time been planning to demolish Silver Street Station, in preparation for a new multistory parking garage."

Meera gasped. Auntie Priya hadn't told her *that!*

"Lonchester City Council would like to

reassure tax payers that there are no plans *whatsoever* to make this site into a city farm."

As he said the words "city farm," he made a face as if, Gemma thought, he'd swallowed a wasp.

"Furthermore," he said, now looking so red that Karl wondered if he might explode, "we have decided to begin the demolition of Silver Street Station tomorrow at nine a.m. Thank you."

Officer Worthing turned off the television. She seemed almost as upset as the children.

"Oh, dear," she said. "Oh, dear. Oh, dear."

Gemma buried her nose in a duckling's comforting fluff, and Karl and Meera held the lambs extra close. Nobody said anything.

"All right," said Sergeant Short. "I'll admit that it doesn't look good . . ."

The children shook their heads in gloomy agreement.

"But, you know what they say. . . ." He winked one of his huge winks. "It's not over till the fat policeman sings."

Chapter
Nine

Sergeant Short and his officers worked to improve the temporary animal pens they had built earlier (Officer Worthing was particularly good with the goats). They carried bales of hay and fetched buckets of water from the fountain so the animals wouldn't go thirsty. They even made the children a sort of tent from silvery emergency blankets so that they could spend the night with their makeshift farm in the park.

Just as the first story about Silver Street Station had spread, so did the news about the mini farm camped out in the park and the city council's promise to demolish Silver Street Station. By early evening, the children were surrounded by a curious crowd and a flock of TV and radio reporters waving cameras and microphones.

In spite of what the city council had said about making Silver Street Station into a parking garage, people still wanted to hear about the children's plans for a city farm. But answering the questions from the interviewers and the crowd made it all seem even sadder. Tomorrow, Silver Street Station would be flattened, no matter what the children's plans had been, and all their newfound animals would be homeless.

"OK, ladies and gents," Sergeant Short said at last, "just one more question, then I think you all need to go home! These young people should get some rest."

The reporter from City Wire TV pushed through the crowds and shoved a big fluffy microphone under Meera's nose.

"I'd like to ask," he said with a nasty sneer, "what's going to happen to all your fine plans when Silver Street Station is demolished tomorrow? Aren't you just some rather foolish children with an even more foolish dream?"

The crowd gasped, and there were even a few quiet *boo*s.

Meera looked up at the reporter. Maybe he was right, she thought. Maybe all this time, ever since Gemma, Karl, and she had been friends, it had all been a silly, hopeless dream.

For the first time in her life, Meera was lost for words; her mouth opened like a goldfish's, but nothing would come out.

"Well," said the reporter smugly. "I think *that's* your answer!"

"Oh, no, it isn't," said Gemma, stepping up to him, ducklings peep-peeping from inside her shirt. "We may be kids, but we aren't foolish. A city farm is a really, *really* good idea."

The crowd murmured its approval.

"And do you know what?" said Karl. His voice wobbled a little, but it was still loud. "Maybe Silver Street Station *won't* be demolished."

"Well said!" cried several people in the crowd.

Meera looked at Karl and Gemma and was suddenly ashamed of giving in so easily. She jumped onto a hay bale so that she was eye to eye with the reporter, and she spoke out so that everyone could hear her.

"Yes," she said. "That's right! Maybe tomorrow morning the people of Lonchester will decide that they don't want *another* parking garage and that they'd *much* rather have a city farm instead!"

The whole crowd exploded with cheering as if they'd been holding it in all along. The reporter scowled and slunk away.

Still standing on her hay bale, Meera could see that her parents, Auntie Nat, and Gemma's brother, Lee, were waiting for them at the back of the crowd. And they were cheering loudest of all.

Chapter Ten

Almost as soon as the pink dawn light touched the tops of the trees at the edge of the park, people began to arrive. Sergeant Short wasn't the least bit surprised. He knew his city, and he knew when something big was going to happen.

At six-thirty he asked Julie to heat some water for tea, then he woke the children, who had spent the night curled up in a nest of hay bales under their silver "tent" with the ducklings and the poodle-lambs.

Meera opened her eyes. She saw the tree-tops, the blue sky, and Sergeant Short's big, beaming face looking down at her.

"Time to meet your supporters," he said. "Told you it wasn't over till the fat policeman sings."

Meera sat up and rubbed her eyes, then she rubbed them again. This *had* to be a dream. She nudged Gemma and kicked Karl in the leg—harder than she'd meant to out of sheer astonishment.

Beyond the crash barriers, hundreds and hundreds of people of all ages, shapes, and sizes stood quietly waiting. Many carried homemade banners saying SILVER STREET FARM and WE WANT A FARM NOT A PARKING GARAGE, or simply showing pictures of farm animals.

"We've done it!" exclaimed Karl. "We've gotten the whole city behind us!"

"If we arrive at Silver Street Station with this crowd," said Gemma, "*nothing's* going to be demolished!"

Meera climbed onto the hay bales and called out, "Good morning, everybody!" to the crowd.

"Good morning!" they called back. And, as if Meera's "good morning" had flipped a switch, the whole park suddenly seemed to wake up. Everyone began to talk at once. People worked on their banners, drank from thermoses, ate sandwiches, and jumped up and down to warm up in the chilly early morning air.

More and more people began to arrive: Auntie Nat, with a thermos of hot chocolate and homemade rolls to dip in it ("So exciting," she said. "My Karl and his friends all celebrities now, eh?"); Meera's mom and dad and her three little brothers, with a banner attached to the stroller saying SILVER STREET CITY FARM in letters made of aluminum foil; Lee and his friends, dressed up as animals (three chickens, one sheep, and something that might have been a zebra or a tiger or possibly just a striped caterpillar).

Finally, Gemma's dad turned up with his accordian and started singing "Silver Street's a City Farm" to the tune of "Old MacDonald Had a Farm." Lots of people joined in, so Gemma couldn't be embarrassed.

Then Sergeant Short spoke to the crowd through the megaphone.

"Citizens of Lonchester," he began, so sternly that everyone immediately became very quiet. "It is the duty of the Lonchester Police Force to uphold the law. So I must ask you now to leave the park."

There were a few cries of "Shame!" but the Sergeant held up his hand for silence. "However, if you wish to make your way to Silver Street Station, I will be obliged to provide a full police escort to make sure that nobody gets into any trouble."

Only Meera was close enough to see the twinkle in Sergeant Short's eye as he spoke, but the crowd understood anyway.

And that was how Meera, Karl, and Gemma led a procession of ducklings, sheep-poodles, goats, chickens, and cheering Lonchester citizens across the city to Silver Street Station, with twenty police officers as a guard of honor.

Chapter
Eleven

The protesters sang at the top of their voices, all the way from the park.

"Silver Street's a city farm

Ee-i, ee-i, oh!

And on that farm we'll have some sheep

Ee-i, ee-i, oh!"

Gemma's dad's accordian was joined by Mr. Khan's trombone, a pair of cymbals, and some sleigh bells that were being shaken very enthusiastically by the oldest of Meera's little brothers. Even some of the police officers were humming along.

All the people standing outside the gates of Silver Street must have heard them coming for *ages* because the man from the city council, the backhoe drivers, and a whole lot of other people wearing hard hats and fluorescent vests were just standing and staring, frozen to the spot, as the procession came down the street.

The protesters finished the last verse in four-part harmony:

"Silver Street's a city farm

Ee-i, eeeeeee-iiiiiii, ooooooohhhh!"

Mr. Khan added a lovely little trombone solo right at the end, as they all stopped just inches from the workers and the man from the city council in his gray suit.

For a moment, nobody said anything, apart from the lambs who said, "baaaaa," as it was time for another bottle feeding, and the goats who said, "meeeeeh!" because they were fed up with Meera pulling on their leashes, and the ducklings who "peep-peeped" from inside Gemma's T-shirt.

Then, the man from the city council—who was, Karl noticed, already turning red again— cleared his throat. "If you think that all of this *nonsense*," he said, waving his hand at all the people and their banners, "is going to have the *slightest* effect on the council's decision, then think again!" He shoved an official-looking document under Meera's nose. "This demolition notice gives me the right to flatten this ruin *right now*!" he said, adding under his breath with what could only be described as a snarl, "and there's nothing you kids and your *stupid, mindless, ridiculous* protest can do about it!"

"Ah, Councilor Newberry!" said Sashi, popping up out of the crowd with Stewy and his camera at her side. She pushed a microphone under the councilor's nose. "We've got your comments on tape," she said, smiling innocently. "So I was just wondering if you were officially describing all these good people as ridiculous and stupid and—what was it—mindless?"

"Were you?" demanded the crowd.

"I represent many small businesses in the city," said Mr. Khan, "and I'm sure we wouldn't want to be called *stupid*."

"Noooo!" booed the crowd.

"A city farm is a great community project,"

said Meera's mother. "It's very far from mindless or ridiculous."

"That's right!" cheered the crowd.

"In fact," Meera said, "it might be a good idea for you to tear up that demolition notice right now."

"Yes," Gemma added. "And let all these people help us build our very first city farm!"

Councilor Newberry turned as pale as he'd been red. He dropped the piece of paper and opened the locked gates without another word.

Silver Street Station's new future rushed in, and one very happy ex–guard dog ran out, delighted to see his three friends once again.

Chapter Twelve

By the end of the day, the old station was transformed. Roofs were patched, windows had new glass, and there was even running water and electricity in the old stationmaster's office. The lambs had a stall to sleep in and a fenced yard where they could frolick about. The old signal box had been made into a chicken coop, with perches and a nest box to lay eggs in. The goats had been given a rather overgrown enclosure between the old railway tracks and were already doing a good job of eating some of the bigger bushes. Several supermarket carts had been pulled from the canal, but the ducklings hadn't taken a swim. They were too busy being chased about by their new foster mom, a hen named Mavis, who was so motherly that she didn't notice her new children were ducks, not chickens.

It had been an incredible day. But there was one more incredible thing in store. She stepped out of a rickety little camper van, with a sheepdog following right behind her, and marched straight up to the children, who were stacking hay bales outside the lambs' stall in the old waiting room.

"I'm Flora," the girl said in a broad Scottish accent, "and I'm going to manage your farm."

Her mouth was set in straight line, and her bright blue eyes blazed with determination.

"Um . . ." said Meera. "I thought *we'd* manage the farm."

"You can't," Flora said simply, pushing her wild curly black hair out of her eyes. "There's got to be somebody here twenty-four seven. And you'll be back in school in a week or two. What then? No, no, you definitely need me."

"But where will you live?" Karl asked.

"In my van, of course!" said Flora, as if Karl were two years old.

"We can't pay you. . . ." said Gemma.

"Och, don't worry about that. I've money of my own, I don't need anyone else's."

The children looked at one another and smiled.

"Good," said Flora, smiling back. "That's

settled then! Oh, there's just one more thing," she added. "It's my dog here, Flinty. She's lousy with sheep, but she's a first-class chicken herder. Is that OK with you?"

"Fine!" said Karl, laughing.

"Perfect!" said Gemma.

"Flora," said Meera, "I think a sheepdog that herds chickens is going to fit right in."

Welcome to Silver Street Farm!